Grandma Chickenlegs

American edition published in 2000 by Carolrhoda Books, Inc.,
by arrangement with Transworld Publishers Ltd., London, England.

Text copyright © 2000 by Geraldine McCaughrean
Illustrations copyright © 2000 by Moira Kemp

Carolrhoda Books, Inc., a division of The Lerner Publishing Group
241 First Avenue North, Minneapolis, MN 55401 U.S.A.

Website address: www.lernerbooks.com

Library of Congress Cataloging-in-Publication Data

McCaughrean, Geraldine.
Grandma Chickenlegs / by Geraldine McCaughrean : illustrated by Moira Kemp.
p.   cm.
Summary: In this variation of the traditional Baba Yaga story, a young girl must rely
on the advice of her dead mother and her special doll when her wicked stepmother
sends her to get a needle from Grandma Chickenlegs.
ISBN 1-57505-415-9
[1. Folklore—Russia.] I. Kemp, Moira, ill. II. Baba Yaga. English. III. Title.
PZ8.1.M144Gr 1999   398.2'0947'02—dc21   99-19161

Printed in Singapore
1 2 3 4 5 6 – 05 04 03 02 01 00

The witch leapt into the giant grinding bowl and, grabbing the huge pestle, began to propel her magic vessel through the air. Faster than a chariot she flew, while her chicken-legged house ran after her.

"You won't get away from me!" she screamed, as in the distance Tatia came into sight.

However fast Tatia and Drooga ran, they could no more outrun the witch than take flight. When Tatia looked around, she saw the iron teeth gaping, the eyes ablaze…

"Throw down the towel that Dog gave you!" cried Drooga. At once the towel stretched itself along the ground, a wide rushing river full of sharp rocks, with steep banks and white-water rapids.

The river's magic was too strong for birds or witches to fly over it, and Grandma Chickenlegs had to land her grinding bowl and climb out.

She got down on her knees and began to drink. *Slurp* went the water through those iron teeth. *Gurgle* went the river down Grandma Chickenlegs' throat.

"Rivers won't save you!" she screamed as she leapt back aboard her magic bowl.

Soon she had Tatia in sight again, and almost within her grasp…

"Throw down the comb that Cat gave you!" cried Drooga. And up sprang pine trees— hundreds and thousands of dense, dark pine trees, their trunks so close together that not a weasel could have squeezed between them.

Flying too fast to stop, the magic grinding bowl crashed into the trees and Grandma Chickenlegs fell out on her head.

Like a headless chicken she danced with uncontrollable temper. Her voice screeched over the treetops: "Forests won't save you!"

Baring her iron teeth, she began to chomp and chew on the tree trunks, spitting out twigs and splinters.

But her teeth were wet from drinking the river. Long before the forest was eaten, the iron between her jaws began to rust, and Grandma Chickenlegs had to give up her chase.

When her cottage came trotting along, she went inside it and slammed the door, and the rickety-rackety shack ran off on its four chicken legs, to another country, another story, another secret corner of the tall-tale world.

T atia was still running though, running without looking back, or looking where she was going. She ran—*oof!*—right into a merchant leading his horse along the road.

"Tatia?"

"Daddy!" cried Tatia, and she hugged her father and told him everything just as it had happened.

When they got home, Tatia's father took the scissors from Tatia's sewing basket and called to his new wife and her two daughters. He cut their fine silk dresses from neck to hem, and their six cotton petticoats, too. Then he turned them out of the house in nothing but their underclothes and told them never to come back.

"But we must have clothes!" they wailed.

"Then you had best go and borrow a needle from Grandma Chickenlegs," said Tatia and firmly shut the door.